the hallowed horse

For my father,
William Morris Hunt II

the hallowed horse

A FOLKTALE FROM INDIA

ADAPTED AND ILLUSTRATED BY

demi

DODD, MEAD & COMPANY · NEW YORK

a long time ago in India, there was a young king who had elephants and peacocks, white tigers and black lions, rubies and diamonds. But he did not have a Hallowed Horse.

And *what*, you may ask, is a Hallowed Horse? A rare treasure indeed! He has been endowed by the angels above with wisdom and courage, majesty and victory; and he will give these qualities to his rider. His beautiful white coat is as smooth as moonstone, his mane flashes like a breaking wave, from his feet dance plumes of fire, and his voice resounds like a trumpet of gold.

The king announced that he would give a mountain of rubies to whomever could find such a horse. For he knew that only a Hallowed Horse could protect his kingdom from Kaliya, the Multi-Headed Snake — the most dreadful and hated creature of all.

Out in the country there was a man who raised horses for a living, and one fine spring day he decided to sell them in the marketplace. But on the way, a mare had a pure white foal. All the other horses immediately slowed their pace and then they completely stopped.

"This is trouble!" thought the horseman. "First the birth of the foal stops everything, and now he's already kicking up his heels! He is much too frisky, and will probably start biting people next. I will sell him to the first person who passes by."

But no one would buy the little foal.

"No thank you!" they said. "Your little horse is quite a kicker, and a biter too! He is a holy terror!"

Soon everyone had heard of the "terrible" little foal.

All except for one man, an absent-minded potter. He hadn't heard anything. But when he saw the little foal, the strangest thing happened. The lively little colt danced way out in front of all the other horses, frolicked right up to the potter and began nuzzling his cheek!

The horseman was afraid the foal might bite the poor potter's ear off, or knock him to the ground, breaking all his pots. But instead, the foal was licking the potter's hand, as if he were a pet dog.

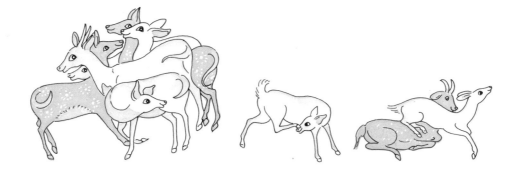

Seizing the moment, the horseman said, "Good sir, I am all out of pots and need every one that you have. For them, I will trade you my favorite little foal, though I can hardly bear to part with him."

The potter felt an instinctive attachment to the playful little horse, and so agreed.

As frisky as he was, the little foal showed exceptional care while moving about the potter's cottage. He gingerly stepped around the pots and never broke one of them.

One day when the potter went out to get some clay, the foal trotted right after him. When he saw his master's sack was full with heavy clay, he offered his back to carry it home.

The potter thought, "What an intelligent and thoughtful animal! I ought to build him a stable." This he did. He also fed him very well. Gradually the little foal grew into a wonderfully fine horse.

Meanwhile, in the king's court, no one had yet been able to find a Hallowed Horse. A dozen astrologers were called upon to help, for it was feared that Kaliya the Multi-Headed Snake was approaching. The astrologers prayed to the stars and the moon, chanted verses, and waved incense, but still there was no sign of a Hallowed Horse. As a last resort, they decided to look into a crystal ball. There, in the dim center, appeared the image of a horse as white as moonstone, with plumes of fire dancing from his feet.

"There he is!" cried the astrologers. "Destined to be a leader of hundreds! But how shall we find him?"

They looked deeper into the crystal ball and saw a potter loading clay onto the back of a most magnificent horse.

"There he is again!" they all cried. "We will visit every potter in the land until we find him!"

It did not take long to find the right potter, who was most astonished to see twelve Royal Astrologers on his humble doorstep. He was even more amazed when they said they wanted to buy his horse at any price.

Now the potter did not wish to sell his horse. And even if he did, he had no idea what price to ask. So he excused himself and went to the stable, quite unsettled, to think things over. But suddenly the silence was broken.

"Ask for anything you like!" said his horse in a deep voice. You can imagine how startled the potter was – a talking horse! All he could do was stare with his mouth open.

His horse continued gently, "Do not be alarmed for I am a Hallowed Horse, destined to serve the king. And do not be sad, my friend, for every year I will come back to you for a long visit."

The poor potter realized that the situation was far beyond his control, so he put his arms around his friend's neck and said goodbye.

The potter and his horse returned to the Royal Astrologers who were eagerly awaiting an answer, but still the potter was too stunned to speak. So the Hallowed Horse stepped forward and said, "This potter, who cared so lovingly for me, will have a mountain of clay and the best potter's wheel in the land. He will have a powerful ox and a magnificent cart to carry his wares to the marketplace. And to keep him company, he will have stables filled with horses and buffaloes, sheep and goats, chickens and roosters!"

In an instant, so many animals appeared that the potter was too distracted to notice that his friend had already left.

The entrance of the Hallowed Horse into the Royal Court was
magnificent. He was given a red and gold saddle and silver shoes
to wear, and around his neck were placed garlands of flowers.
Trumpets blew, silken flags flew, and an army of men on horses and
elephants stood by to salute the Hallowed Horse. When the young
king stepped forward and mounted his steed, everyone went wild
with joy.

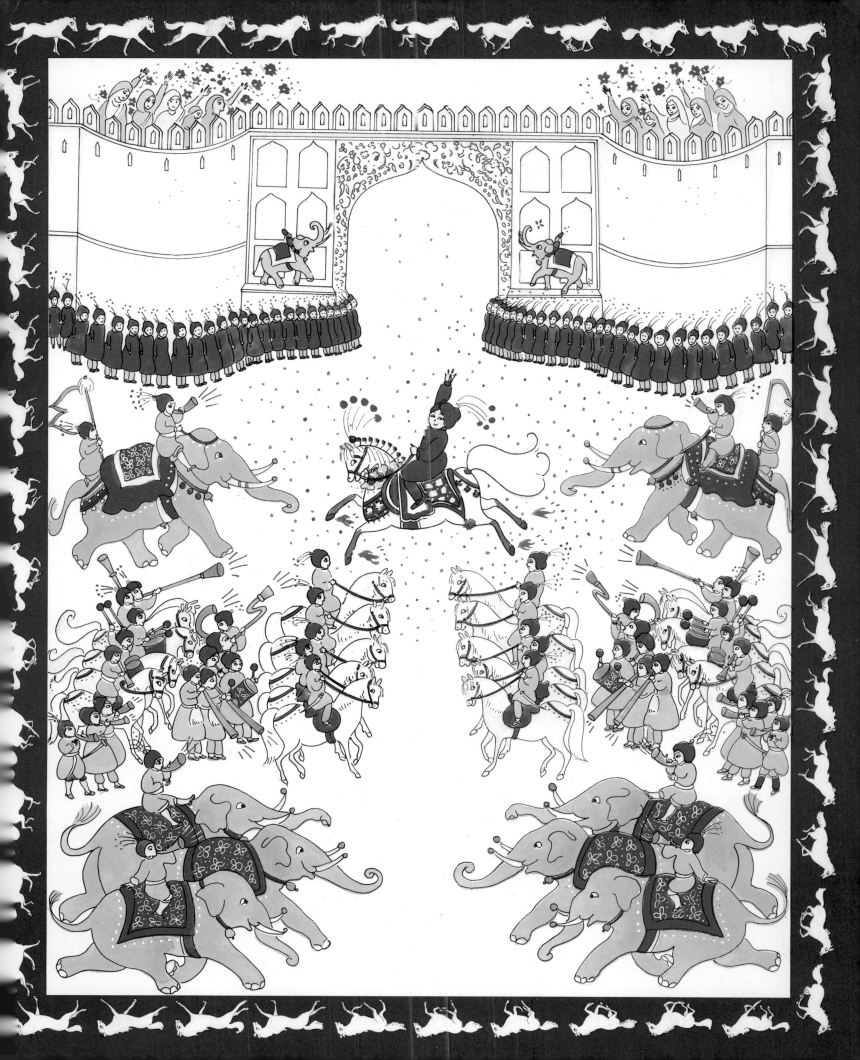

But at that very moment, Kaliya the Multi-Headed Snake had arrived at the city gates with his own army of five hundred hissing snakes riding on the backs of five hundred horses!

The young king and his horse immediately shot out like an arrow to confront the great enemy. Suddenly, the Hallowed Horse stopped, reared up on his hind legs, and with a mighty sound like a trumpet call, whinnied loudly.

In response to the call of their *true* leader, Kaliya's five hundred horses began neighing and bucking. They threw off their hissing snake riders and trampled them to death. Kaliya had lost his evil army and was forced to retreat to the mountains far beyond the kingdom, completely vanquished!

To celebrate the great victory and peace at last, the king declared the day to be a sacred holiday. The whole kingdom resounded with cries of "LONG LIVE THE KING! LONG LIVE THE HALLOWED HORSE!" Peacocks waved flowers in their beaks, black lions and white tigers leaped for joy, while all the horses and elephants danced!

The first kings in the old Indian legends were heavenly. They in turn bequeathed their magic powers to their mortal counterparts. An Indian king, therefore, was not only a military leader, but had been given divine sanction.

The story of the Hallowed Horse tells of an Indian king who is magically blessed with a divine horse that roots out all evil and restores the forces of good.

Design and art direction by Barbara DuPree Knowles

1 2 3 4 5 6 7 8 9 10

LIBRARY OF CONGRESS CATALOGING-IN-PUBLICATION DATA

Demi. – The hallowed horse. – *Summary:* The young king of India searches for a Hallowed Horse to protect his kingdom from the evil Kaliya, the Multi-Headed Snake.
  [1. Fairy tales.   2. Folklore – India]   I. Title.   PZ8.D3994Hal   1987
398.2′2′0954 [E]   87-6797   ISBN 0-396-08908-9